How Raven Brought Light to People

How Raven Brought Light to People

retold by Ann Dixon

illustrated by James Watts

MARGARET K. McELDERRY BOOKS
New York

Maxwell Macmillan Canada / Maxwell Macmillan International
Toronto / New York Oxford Singapore Sydney

Margaret K. McElderry Books
Macmillan Publishing Company
866 Third Avenue
New York, NY 10022

Maxwell Macmillan Canada, Inc.
1200 Eglinton Avenue East
Suite 200
Don Mills, Ontario M3C 3N1

Macmillan Publishing Company is part of the Maxwell Communication Group of Companies.

First edition
Printed in Hong Kong
Book design by James Watts and Nancy B. Williams
The text of this book is set in Tiffany Light.
The illustrations are watercolor and acrylic on illustration board.
10 9 8 7 6 5 4 3 2 1

Library of Congress Cataloging-in-Publication Data
Dixon, Ann.
How Raven brought light to people / retold by Ann Dixon ; illustrated by
James Watts.— 1st ed.
p.   cm.
Summary: Raven gives the sun, the moon, and the stars to the
people of the world by tricking the great chief who is hoarding them
in three boxes.
ISBN 0-689-50536-1
1. Tlingit Indians—Legends. 2. Ravens—Folklore. [1. Tlingit
Indians—Legends. 2. Indians of North America—Alaska—Legends.]
I. Watts, James, 1955- ill. II. Title.
E99.T6D59 1992
398.2'089972—dc20   90-28948

To the Story Hour children at the Willow Public Library.
Thank you for listening.
—A.D.

For my daughter, Alytė
—J.W.

Long ago when the earth was new,
so new that people had no sun or moon or stars for light, there
lived a great chief who had three beautiful wooden boxes.

Raven heard talk that the great chief kept the sun, the moon, and the stars in these wooden boxes. He thought it was wrong for the chief to hide the lights where no one could see them.

The more he thought about it, the madder he got.

Raven grew exceedingly tired of so much darkness. One day (or perhaps it was night) as Raven sat by a deep, still pool in the river scheming over ways to get at the sun, the moon, and the stars, a young woman came to bathe.

He could tell by the song she sang that she was the daughter of the great chief.

Quick as a splash, an idea came to him.

He changed himself into a tiny spruce needle and dropped into the young woman's hands as she scooped up a drink from the river.

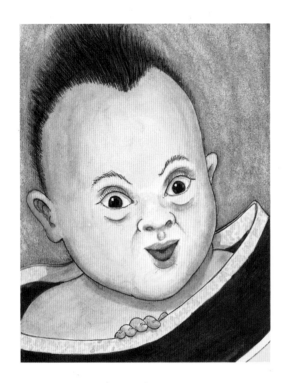

Once the girl swallowed the needle, Raven turned himself into a baby and surprised everyone by being born.

The great chief grew to love the boy deeply, and he noticed that the child's eyes were unusually bright and quick.

One especially dark, dreary day, this boy-who-was-Raven could stand it no longer. He reached for the three wooden boxes that were up on a shelf and started to cry.

Nothing the chief or his daughter or those who served them could do would quiet him.

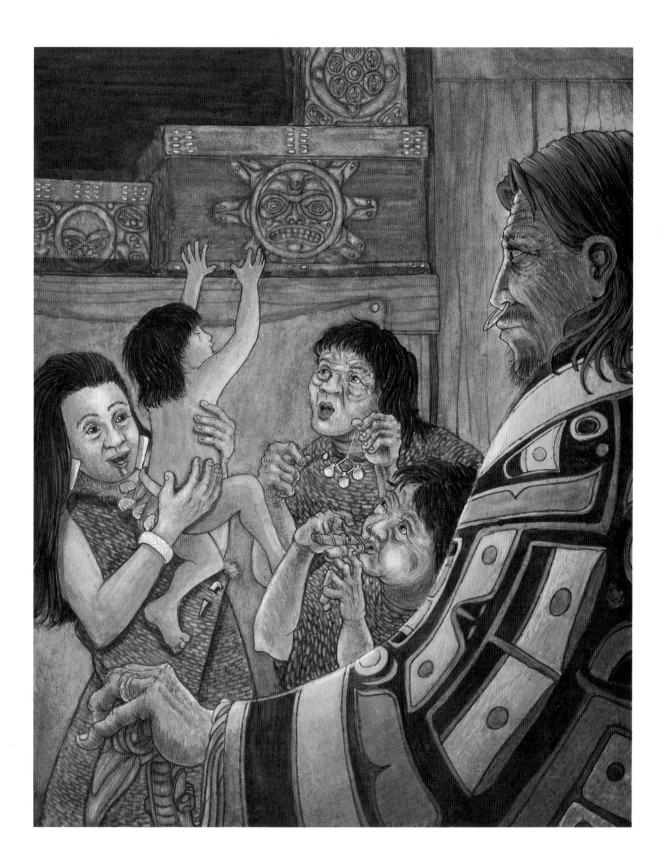

Finally the chief gave his grandson the box with the stars inside. "You may look at the box," he told Raven, "but do not open the lid!"

Raven played happily with the box until no one was looking. And then . . . he opened the lid.

Up flew the stars—to the top of the lodge and out through the smoke-hole.

They rose high into the sky, filling the heavens with millions
of sparkling lights.

Seeing the stars, people said to each other, "What beautiful little lights we have now!"

At first the great chief felt sad that his stars were gone.

But Raven smiled so sweetly that the old man forgave him almost immediately.

It wasn't long, however, before Raven wanted more light than the stars alone could provide. Once again he reached for the boxes on the shelf and started to cry.

Nothing the chief or his daughter or those who served them could do would quiet him.

Finally the chief said with a sigh, "I suppose that now I must give you the box with the moon to play with or you will never stop crying!"

And he gave the box to the boy.

Raven played with the box, then took the moon out and pretended it was a ball.

For a while the servants watched him roll the ball.

But as soon as they stopped watching . . .

Raven tossed the moon up and out through the smoke-hole in the top of the lodge.

It floated up into the sky between the earth and the stars, shedding a great light on the world.

Seeing the moon, people said to each other, "This moon looks
beautiful next to the stars!"

But the old chief felt twice as sad, for now his moon and stars were both gone.

Still he didn't grow angry with Raven, for when the boy reached out to him, calling, "Grandfather!" the chief knew he loved the boy more than all his wonderful possessions.

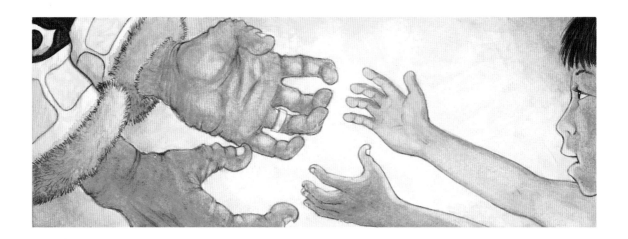

The moon and the stars didn't satisfy Raven for long, however. The most brilliant light in the world still rested within the chief's last wooden box.

So one day he reached for the last wooden box on the shelf and started to cry.

But this time the chief ignored the boy, until finally Raven cried himself sick.

Raven was so ill that he could not eat or drink.

At last the boy's mother ran to the chief and started crying, too. "Father," she said, "you see that my son will die if he doesn't stop crying. He won't stop crying unless you give him that box. If you don't give him the box he will surely die. What good are treasures if your grandson is lost?"

The wisdom of his daughter's words spoke to the great chief's heart.

"Give the box to the boy," he instructed his servants.

"But don't open the lid," he warned Raven severely, "or the light will burn your eyes."

Raven played happily with the box for several days while the servants kept watch.

But at last the servants grew careless and fell to talking.

In an instant the boy seized the box and turned into Raven once again. He flew toward the smoke-hole to escape.

Suddenly, the chief realized that Raven had tricked him.

He quickly cast a spell to shrink the smoke-hole shut.

Still holding the box, Raven pushed with his head and poked with his beak and rubbed with his shoulders against the sooty smoke-hole, until at last . . .

he was able to squeeze through.

But because of the chief's magic the soot clung to Raven, turning him black from head to tail. And ever since all ravens have been black.

Raven flew far up into the sky to set free the sun. As he lifted the lid a tremendous noise erupted, more powerful than thunder, and the sun vaulted into the heavens.

And from that day to this, the sun, the moon, and the stars

have shone on all the people of the earth.

7/04 X7